GARDENING WITH PETER RABBIT

Text by Jennie Walters

WITH NEW REPRODUCTIONS FROM THE ORIGINAL ILLUSTRATIONS BY

BEATRIX POTTER ™

F. WARNE & Co.

Acknowledgements

Most of the illustrations by Beatrix Potter in this book come from her Peter Rabbit Tales published
by Frederick Warne. Other drawings by Beatrix Potter are reproduced by courtesy of the following:
The National Art Library, Victoria and Albert Museum - pages 12 (left), 13 (right), 14 (left),
27 (left), 28 (right), 30 (left) and 43;
The Trustees of the Linder Collection, Book Trust - page 29 (right)

All other illustrations and diagrams are by Rowan Clifford

FREDERICK WARNE

Published by the Penguin Group
27 Wrights Lane, London W8 5TZ, England
Penguin Books USA Inc., 375 Hudson Street, New York, N.Y. 10014, USA
Penguin Books Australia Ltd, Ringwood, Victoria, Australia
Penguin Books Canada Ltd, 10 Alcorn Avenue, Toronto, Ontario, Canada M4V 3B2
Penguin Books (N.Z.) Ltd, 182-190 Wairau Road, Auckland 10, New Zealand

Penguin Books Ltd, Registered Offices: Harmondsworth, Middlesex, England

First published 1992
5 7 9 10 8 6

ISBN 0 7232 3998 3

Colour reproduction by Anglia Graphics Ltd, Bedford
Printed and bound in Great Britain by William Clowes Limited,
Beccles and London

CONTENTS

Introduction

There are lots of gardens and gardeners in the stories about Peter Rabbit and his friends. Peter squeezed under the gate into Mr. McGregor's garden to eat the vegetables there, and when he grew up, he kept a nursery garden himself. Tom Kitten and his sisters got into all sorts of trouble in an old-fashioned garden, filled with cottage flowers. Timmy Willie, the little

From *The Tale of Johnny Town-Mouse*

From *The Tale of Tom Kitten*

country mouse in *The Tale of Johnny Town-Mouse*, was born in a garden, which he missed dreadfully when taken to town in a hamper of vegetables: '. . . you should see my garden and the flowers – roses and pinks and pansies – no noise except the birds and the bees, and the lambs in the meadows.' And Jemima Puddle-duck went around the farm garden, nibbling off snippets of the herbs that are

From *The Tale of Jemima Puddle-Duck*

well. All most plants need is soil, light and water. When a seed is warm and watered, it begins to grow; this is called 'germination'. Then its roots take food from the soil, while sunshine helps the plant turn water and air into food for its leaves and stem. It is wonderful to see shoots springing up from the soil and, if you grow some bulbs or seeds in glass jars, you can watch the roots sprouting downwards as well.

used for stuffing roast duck.

Gardens are homes to all sorts of creatures: birds, bees, butterflies, mice, frogs, and lots more. Sweet-smelling plants like lilac and lavender will encourage butterflies to come, and a bird table with some scraps and a dish of water will help look after the birds in cold weather. Some sprays and weedkillers, on the other hand, may be harmful to bees and other insects.

You don't need to have a garden outdoors to enjoy growing flowers and plants, though: a pot on a sunny window-sill can start you off just as

From *The Tale of Mrs. Tittlemouse*

From *The Tale of The Flopsy Bunnies*

To be a good indoor gardener, you should:
● make sure your plants don't dry out, but be careful not to over-water them. Tepid water is better than cold, and rainwater is best of all for most plants – not cacti. (Keep a bucket outside to catch the rain.)
● keep your plants away from cold and draughts, but also away from direct heat from a fire or radiator.
● transfer your plants to a bigger container, adding more compost, if their roots begin to grow through the holes in the bottom of the flowerpot.
● gently turn over the topsoil around the plants with a stick or fork from time to time, so that it doesn't get mouldy, and replace most of the soil after several months.
● spread out plenty of old newspapers if you are working with compost or soil, so that you don't make too much mess.

To be a good outdoor gardener, you should:
● make sure your plants don't get smothered by weeds. Sometimes it's difficult to tell which is which when the plants are small, so you may have to wait till they've grown some more leaves.
● water your plants well in dry weather, but do it when the sun has gone down, so that all the water doesn't evaporate straight away.
● pick any dead flowers from their stalks, so that the plant can use all its strength to make new blooms.
● protect your young seedlings from garden pests. Cutting the bottom off a plastic drinks bottle, and then slicing it into three rings will give you individual fences to keep out slugs and snails, or you could try just putting a ring of salt around the plants. Wash

the leaves with soapy water if you spot greenfly or blackfly.

Tools and other things to collect
Many of the projects in this book only require very simple tools and ingredients. Keep an eye out for the following things:

Old kitchen knives, forks and spoons for indoor gardening, plus a pair of scissors for trimming plants. A pencil is also useful as a 'dibber' – to make a hole in compost in which to

From *The Tale of Peter Rabbit*

From *The Tale of Peter Rabbit*

sow your seed.

A trowel, a rake and a small garden fork will be needed for gardening outside, and a spade if you need to do some heavy digging. Ask your parents before borrowing or using these tools.

A fine watering-can, for watering seedlings, or a pump-action spray container (the sort which may have held window-cleaner, for example), rinsed out thoroughly.

Flowerpots in clay or plastic (remember to soak new clay flowerpots in water for an hour, or they'll be too dry), or any other containers which will hold soil, such as margarine tubs, yogurt cartons and foil trays from ready-made dishes. You'll need to make a few holes in the

From *Cecily Parsley's Nursery Rhymes*

bottom of these so that the water can drain away and won't rot the plant roots.

Peat pots, which you can buy from a garden centre or hardware shop. They are much better for tiny seedlings than plastic containers, as moisture and air can circulate through them. You can also transplant the peat pots straight into a bigger flowerpot as the seedling grows, without having to disturb it.

Broken china or pebbles to put in the bottom of your flowerpots, which will make it even easier for the water to drain from the soil.

Glass jars in various sizes, with and without lids, and vases, for growing bulbs in water and making bottle gardens.

Old saucers or trays to stand the pots and containers on.

Compost and sand for your indoor plants to grow in (these will feed them better than earth from the garden). You can buy compost especially for young seedlings from garden centres. They will also sell washed sand.

Charcoal, in small pieces, which you can put in large plant containers, bulb jars or bottle gardens to help keep them fresh (charcoal absorbs unwanted water and harmful gases). You can buy it from pet shops, homecare stores or garden centres.

A few straight sticks in case you need to support a straggling plant.

PROJECTS
FOR SPRING

Indoor Herbs

(March to April)

You will need:

Seed trays, or foil containers from ready-made dishes (one for each type of herb)
Potting compost for seedlings (such as John Innes No. 1)
A pump-action sprayer, well-rinsed if necessary
Herb seeds (try basil, thyme, mint or chives)
An old kitchen fork
Strips cut from margarine or yogurt pots, for labels
A ball-point pen
Adhesive tape
Clear plastic bags, big enough to cover the seed trays
Rubber bands or wire tie-fasteners
Peat pots, or empty yogurt or margarine tubs
A pencil, to use as a 'dibber'
A long plastic or foil tray
Flowerpots, with pebbles in the bottom for drainage

Fill your seed tray or container with compost, and make little furrows along it with your finger, for the seeds to be sown in. Water the compost well with the sprayer, then sow your

'She also sold herbs, and rosemary tea, and rabbit-tobacco (which is what *we* call lavender).'
From *The Tale of Benjamin Bunny*

chosen seed carefully along the furrows, following the instructions on the packet. Sow one type of seed per tray.

Gently fork a thin layer of compost over the seeds, then water them again. Write the name of the seed on your label and tape it to the tray.

Put the tray into a plastic bag and close it with an elastic band or tie. Leave it in a warm place for a week or so.

When the seedlings have started to grow, take the tray out of the plastic bag and leave it on the window-sill for a while longer. Water the plants well, and make sure they're not in a draught.

When the seedlings have grown a first pair of leaves, and then another leaf after that, move the strongest plants into peat or yogurt pots so that they have more room to grow (this is called 'pricking out'). If using peat pots, soak them in water and then fill them with compost. (Don't separate the pots, or they won't stand up.) If using yogurt tubs, simply fill them with compost. Make one or two holes in the compost of each pot with your pencil dibber.

Using the fork, carefully separate your seedlings. Choose good strong ones and, holding them gently by the bottom leaves (not the stem), position them in the peat or yoghurt pots. Firm the compost carefully around each plant with your dibber.

Group the pots of herbs together along a tray and place them on a sunny window-sill. Keep them well watered and, when the seedlings are about 5–6 cm (about 2 in) high, or you notice roots growing out through the bottom of the peat pots, transplant them to larger flowerpots.

Put pebbles or crocks in the bottom of the pots to help drainage, add a good layer of compost, then either put in the whole peat pot and plant, or carefully tip out your plant from the yogurt pot and place it in a hollow in the compost. Fill up with more compost, firm it up round the plant and then water.

TIP: You don't have to worry about watering seedlings so often if you have sealed them in a plastic bag after their first watering. This is because the warmth makes moisture from the damp compost rise up as condensation, and when it meets the cold plastic covering, it turns back to water again. Just flick the bag if you see water appearing on the inside, to stop the seedlings rotting.

A Flower Garden
(March to May – look at your seed packets)

You will need:

A sunny spot in the garden
A small garden fork
A rake
Some large stones for edging, if you like (you may find these in the garden, on a seashore, or even in a skip)
Flower seeds – choose hardy annuals such as nasturtiums, clarkia, candytuft, marigolds or nigella (some companies make special collections of seeds for children)

Watercolour of nasturtiums by Beatrix Potter

Some lollipop sticks
A pen
A fine watering-can
A trowel

From *Cecily Parsley's Nursery Rhymes*

First choose the site for your flower garden. Ask your parents if there is a sunny corner of the garden where they will let you plant your seeds.

Fork over the soil to break it up and move away any large stones. Then rake the soil so that it is fine and your plant roots will be able to push their way through easily. Water it if it is dry. If you like, make a border around your flower garden with some large stones.

Have a good look at your seed packets, to find out how and where to sow your seeds. You'll want to put the tallest flowers at the back, and the shortest at the front. Don't sow too many seeds; two or three types of

12

flower may be enough, and you don't have to use all the seeds in the packet. Hardy annuals will only last for one season, but they are quite strong and easy to grow.

From *The Tale of The Pie and The Patty-Pan*

Write the name of your flowers on a lollipop stick and place it near each variety, so that you can remember what you have sown.

Water your seeds again two days after planting and every few days after that, if the soil is dry. When your seedlings have grown about two or three proper leaves, take out the weaker-looking plants so that the others have plenty of room to grow (check your seed packets again to see how much room to give them). This is called 'thinning out'.

Make sure the soil doesn't dry out as your flowers appear, and dig up any weeds with your fork or a trowel. Pinch off any dead or faded flowers, too. This will keep the plant strong and encourage more blooms to come.

TIP: Don't throw your seed packets away, even if you have used all the seeds. Keep them to refer to later on, when you have to start taking out some seedlings so the others have room to grow.

Tortoiseshell butterfly by Beatrix Potter

A Blossoming Branch

(March to May – look at your seed packets)

A blossoming branch by Beatrix Potter

You will need:

A piece of bamboo, about 30 cm (1 ft) long
A craft knife
Sheets of newspaper
Flower seeds – choose annuals, such as nasturtiums, marigolds, cornflowers, candytuft
Potting compost for seeds (such as John Innes No. 1)
Cotton thread
Scissors
A flowerpot, with pebbles in the bottom for drainage
A saucer, to stand your flowerpot on

Ask an adult to help you split the bamboo in half along its length with the knife, resting on several sheets of newspaper. Take out any pith there might be.

Place your flower seeds along one half section of bamboo, at about 2½ cm (1 in) intervals.

Mix the compost with a little water to make a paste, and spread this paste along both halves of bamboo. Place the two halves back together and tie them – loosely – at three or four places with the thread.

Push one end of the bamboo into a pot filled with compost on top of drainage pebbles, and stand the pot on a saucer. Water the pot and the twig once a week. In a few weeks, the flowers will start to push their way out of the twig and bloom all along the branch in summer.

Potatoes in a Pot
(February to March)

You will need:

A large flowerpot
Some pebbles or broken china
Potting compost, or earth from the
    garden with some handfuls of peat
    mixed in
A potato which has begun to sprout
    white shoots (this is called a 'tuber')
Old newspapers

Prepare your flowerpot by putting a layer of broken china or pebbles in the bottom. This will make sure the roots of your potato plant don't block the holes in the bottom of the pot and stop the water from draining away. Then fill the pot about three-quarters full of compost or earth and peat.

Choose an earthy potato with some white sprouts that are not too long – about 1.5 cm (¾ in) is just right. Put it in the pot with the sprouts uppermost and cover it with another thick layer of compost or earth. Don't fill the pot right up, as you'll need to add more compost or earth as the plant grows.

Press the soil down gently, water the plant well and put it somewhere there is plenty of light. Water the plant again whenever the soil dries

From *Cecily Parsley's Nursery Rhymes*

out: check it every few days.

TIP: Always stand your flowerpots or other containers on an old saucer or a tray. This will stop water leaking out through the drainage holes onto your window-sill or floor, and catch the water so it doesn't run straight through your pot.

15

From *Cecily Parsley's Nursery Rhymes*

When shoots and leaves begin to appear, add more compost or earth mixture to the pot, leaving about 2.5 cm (1 in) of the stem showing. This is to stop light reaching the new potatoes and turning them green, and is called 'earthing up'.

You should see small white flowers appearing on your plant. When the first one has died, it's time to harvest your crop (probably about 10 weeks after planting). Turn the pot upside down on some newspaper and pick off the new potatoes. Ask an adult to help you boil them, and eat them with butter – delicious!

Window-sill tomatoes
(January to July – see your seed packet)

You will need:

Peat pots
Potting compost for seeds (such as
    John Innes No. 1)
Tomato seeds – be sure to choose a
    dwarf variety suitable for growing
    in pots, such as Tiny Tim or Minibel
A small tray or large plate
A clear plastic bag, big enough to
    cover the tray or plate
A rubber band or wire tie-fastener
A fine watering-can or pump-action
    sprayer, well-rinsed if necessary
A mixture of 2 parts soil to 1 of peat,
    or compost for larger plants (such as
    John Innes No. 3)
Large flowerpots, with pebbles in the
    bottom for drainage
A tray or box to stand your flowerpots
    on
Liquid fertiliser
Sticks or other supports for your plant

First of all, soak your peat pots in water, then fill them with compost for seeds. (Don't separate the pots, or they won't stand up.) Put two seeds in each pot, then cover with a thin layer of compost.

Water the seeds well with tepid

From *The Tale of Peter Rabbit*

flowerpot. Fill the pots with a layer of compost for plants (over the drainage pebbles), such as John Innes No. 3, place the whole peat pot in and fill up with more compost. Firm the soil round the plant and water it well.

When you see small green tomatoes on your plants, feed them with liquid fertiliser (follow the instructions on the bottle or packet carefully to make it up). Tie the plants to sticks if they start to flop about.

> TIP: Tomatoes need lots of sunshine, and will grow best on a south-facing window-sill.

water, then stand the pots on a tray or plate and put the whole thing in a large plastic bag. Fasten it with a rubber band or wire tie.

Leave the tray in a warm place for the seeds to germinate. When the seedlings start to show, take off the plastic bag. Remove the weaker-looking seedling from each pot, being careful not to harm the roots of the other.

Water the peat pots often, whenever the compost dries out.

When the seedlings are about 6 cm (2½ in) high and you see roots growing out of the pots, it is time to transfer the whole peat pot to a larger

From *The Tale of The Flopsy Bunnies*

17

Crunchy Radishes

(March to September, though radishes grown in a dry July and August may be too peppery)

You will need:

A small garden fork
Some peat
A rake
A watering-can
A pencil 'dibber'
A packet of radish seeds (choose
    summer varieties such as French
    Breakfast and Scarlet Globe)
A lollipop stick
A ballpoint pen

Radishes are easy and quick to grow (they should be ready to eat about a month after you've sown them), and are delicious eaten dipped in salt or with a little butter.

Choose a sunny spot in the garden to sow your radish seeds in spring, or plant them in the shade of some other plants if sowing in summer. Dig the soil over with your fork, taking away any large stones, and fork in some peat as well.

Rake the soil well and make furrows with your dibber, about 1 cm (½ in) deep and 15 cm (6 in) apart. Sow your seeds very thinly, about 1 seed every 2 cm (1 in), and cover them over with finely raked soil.

Water the seed furrows well, and water the seedlings again every few days in dry weather – whenever the soil dries out.

After about four weeks, pull up one of the plants to see if your radishes are ready for eating. Don't let them grow too big: about 1 cm (½ in) across is the right sort of size.

From the privately printed edition
The Tale of Peter Rabbit

18

From *The Tale of Peter Rabbit*

From *The Peter Rabbit Diary*

PROJECTS
FOR SUMMER

From *The Tale of*
Johnny Town-Mouse

Tiny Fruit Trees
(throughout the spring and summer)

'When it rains, I sit in my little sandy burrow
and shell corn and seeds from my
Autumn store.'
From *The Tale of Johnny Town-Mouse*

You will need:

Some small flowerpots
Potting compost
Grapefruit, orange and lemon pips
Plastic bags
Rubber bands
A few peanuts in their shells
A fine watering-can or sprayer, well-
 rinsed if necessary
An orange or grapefruit
A sharp knife
A thin knitting needle or skewer
A pencil, for a 'dibber'

Plants don't only grow from packets of seeds that you have to buy; you can also raise tiny trees from all sorts of pips and nuts. They won't bear fruit, but they may flower, and you can plant them in a miniature garden later (see page 38).

Try orange or lemon pips, which you can then plant in orange or grapefruit halves. Fill some small flowerpots nearly to the brim with potting compost, and plant three orange or lemon pips per pot. Water the pots well and put a plastic bag over each one, securing it round the pot with a rubber band. Keep them in a warm place, like an airing cupboard.

Plant peanuts in the same way. Gently crack their shells, being careful not to damage the nut inside, and plant them three to a pot.

When you see shoots appear (about three weeks later for fruit pips, or one week for peanut plants), bring the

Peanut plant

You may be able to get new nuts from your peanut plant. After its flowers have faded, the stalks may push down into the compost to produce new nuts. It won't need watering quite so often now.

pots into the light. Keep them in their polythene bags until the second pair of leaves grows.

Then re-plant the strongest seedlings in their own pots, or in orange or grapefruit halves, which look very pretty. Cut the fruit in half, then ask an adult to help you scoop out all the flesh.

Pierce holes in the skin with the knitting needle or skewer and fill the half-fruit with compost. Make a hole in the compost with your dibber and put in your plant, firming the compost around it. Water well and keep the plants on a sunny window-sill.

If roots appear through the bottom of the fruit container, simply plant the whole thing in a larger flowerpot, full of compost.

Why not try growing a plant from an avocado stone, too (this works best in later summer). Soak the stone in warm water for a day or so to soften it, then push in four toothpicks or cocktail sticks towards the narrow end of the stone. Balance it over a jar of water, so that the wide end is right in the water. When you see thick white roots (after about 6 to 8 weeks), plant the stone in its own flowerpot of compost on the window-sill.

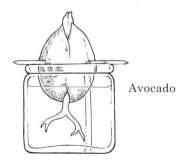

Avocado

Carrot Ferns and a Pineapple Plant

(throughout the spring and summer)

From *Appley Dapply's Nursery Rhymes*

You will need:

Some carrots (those which have
    started to sprout at the top will
    almost certainly grow into ferns)
A sharp knife
Some saucers
A fresh pineapple
3 or 4 flowerpots
Potting compost
Drainage pebbles
A fine watering-can or sprayer, well-
rinsed if necessary
A little clean sand
A clear plastic bag
A rubber band

To grow your carrot ferns, carefully slice the tops off, about 1½ cm (¾ in) from the end. Place each carrot top in a saucer of water. A week or so later, a pretty green fern will start to grow, though it won't develop any roots. Keep topping up the water in the saucer, so it doesn't all evaporate.

To start your pineapple plant, carefully slice the top off a fresh pineapple, about 3 cm (1½ in) from the end, or so that you have the first row of diamond-shaped sections. Be very careful to keep your fingers out of the way of the knife.

Pineapple plant

Keep the pot in a warm, shady place. Within about eight weeks or so, you should find that the plant has started to grow. Take off the plastic bag when new leaves appear and keep your plant in a sunny place, moving it to a larger pot when necessary.

Look for other natural things to grow. Collect acorns in the autumn and keep them outside in damp sand through the winter. Soak them in water for a day, then balance them in the neck of a bottle filled with water and plant them in a pot when their roots have grown. Conkers can be kept in damp sand and then planted straight into damp compost in the spring.

From *Appley Dapply's Nursery Rhymes*

Keep the top for one or two days, to dry off.

Put some drainage pebbles in a flowerpot and fill it nearly to the top with potting compost. Water the compost, then sprinkle on a little sand.

Put the pineapple top on the sand and cover the cut end up with some more compost. Pull a clear plastic bag over the pot and secure it with a rubber band.

25

New Plants from Old

(June to September)

You will need:

A Busy Lizzie (impatiens) plant
Sharp scissors
A jam jar of water
A small flowerpot
Peat or soil mixed with equal
    quantities of clean sand
A pencil 'dibber'
A watering-can or sprayer, well-
    rinsed if necessary

Busy Lizzie cuttings

From *The Tale of Peter Rabbit*

You can have even more plants to brighten the window-sill by taking cuttings from the 'parent' plant and growing them in their own pots. This is much quicker than growing from seed.

Be sure to ask first if you are taking a cutting from someone else's Busy Lizzie. Then cut off a shoot about 10 cm (4 in) long, choosing one which comes from the main stem and has no buds or flowers on it.

Take off the bottom leaves from the cutting, so that they won't rot, trim it just underneath the leaf joint, and put it into a jam jar of water. In a few days' time, it should have grown some roots, and will need to be planted in a pot.

26

Fill a small flowerpot with peat or soil mixed with sand (which helps the water to drain from the soil), and make a hole in the soil with your pencil dibber. Pour in a little water.

Very gently plant the cutting in the hole, taking care not to damage the roots, and firm the soil around it. Water it well.

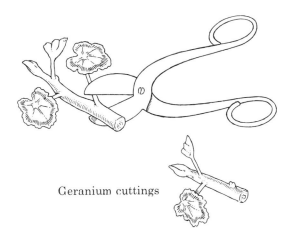

Geranium cuttings

Rabbits' potting shed by Beatrix Potter

You can plant geranium cuttings straight into a pot full of sandy soil or peat. Cut and trim a shoot as described above, put it in a hole you've made in the sandy soil or peat and water it well. Ivy cuttings will grow in oasis, which you can buy from a florist's shop or garden centre. Take an ivy cutting as described above and stick it into some damp oasis in the bottom of a jam jar. When you see roots appearing, you can carefully take out the cutting and plant it in a flowerpot filled with compost.

An Indoor Window-box
(throughout the summer)

From *The Tale of The Flopsy Bunnies*

You will need:

An empty ice-cream or other large
  plastic container, with lid
Stick-on shapes to decorate it, if you
  like
A pair of scissors or metal skewer
Drainage pebbles
Potting compost
Plants, perhaps cuttings you have
  taken, or some bedding plants from
  a garden centre
Twigs, shells, pretty stones and so on,
  for extra interest
A fine watering-can or empty sprayer,
  well-rinsed if necessary
Some Blu-tack or Plasticine

Make sure your container is clean,
then decorate it with stick-on shapes,
if you want. Ask an adult to help you
pierce several holes in the bottom with
the scissors or skewer, for drainage,
add some pebbles, then fill the tub
with compost.

Arrange your plants on the top of
the compost, to see how they look best.
Put low-growing plants at the front
and taller ones behind. Ivy looks
pretty trailing over the edge of the
tub, or you can train it to grow up a
tall twig at the back of the window-
box.

Watercolour of ivy by Beatrix Potter

From *The Tale of The Flopsy Bunnies*

When you think you have got the best arrangement, make hollows in the compost for each plant with your dibber, lower it gently in and firm the compost around it. Water the whole arrangement well.

Roll four small balls of Blu-tack or Plasticine and place one in each corner of the container lid. Balance the planted tub on top, pressing down gently so that it is held quite firmly. This will help water to drain from the tub and stop the plant roots rotting.

You can make several tubs and arrange them along a window-sill to brighten up the room. A planted tub makes a good present, too, especially if you decorate the tub to suit the person it's for. You can cut out their name in sticky-backed plastic, or choose stickers of their favourite character.

A cottage porch by Beatrix Potter

Christmas-present Bulbs
(late August)

You will need:

Bulb fibre, which you can buy from
  garden centres
A bucket of water
A fairly shallow bowl or empty plastic
  container, without drainage holes
Stick-on shapes to decorate a plastic
  container, if you wish

Bulbs, such as daffodil, hyacinth or
  tulip – look on the packet to find
  some which have been specially
  treated to bloom early
A fine watering-can or sprayer, well-
  rinsed if necessary

Soak your bulb fibre overnight in a
bucket of water. Decorate your plastic
container with stick-on shapes, if you
wish.

  Squeeze out the bulb fibre so that
it's moist but not wet, and put a layer
in the bottom of your container or
bowl. Add as many bulbs as you can fit
in the bowl, pointed ends uppermost,
and fill the spaces between them with
more damp bulb fibre. The tops of the
bulbs should just show above the fibre.

Watercolour of daffodils by Beatrix Potter

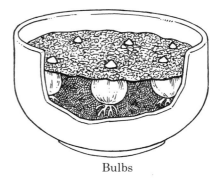

Bulbs

Put the bowl in a cool, dark place –
perhaps a cupboard, or wrapped in a

30

black dustbin liner in the garden shed (the dark helps the bulbs to grow good strong roots). Don't forget to check the bulb fibre from time to time, though, and water it whenever it feels dry.

When you can see about 6 cm (2½ in) of the bulb leaves, move the container to a cool window-sill. It can be brought into the warmth when the shoots are about 10 cm (4 in) high. (The warmth indoors encourages the bulbs to grow more quickly than they would outside.)

Keep watering the bowl, and you should have a beautiful, fresh Christmas present for somebody.

From *The Peter Rabbit Diary*

When the bulbs have finished flowering, cut off the dead flowers, but let the leaves die down by themselves (they feed the bulb so that it will flower again next spring). The bulbs won't flower again indoors, but you can plant them in the garden to bloom once more outside.

You don't need to worry about drainage holes if you fill your containers with bulb fibre; it contains charcoal, which absorbs unwanted water and keeps the fibre fresh.

From *The
Peter Rabbit
Diary*

PROJECTS FOR AUTUMN

From *Cecily Parsley's Nursery Rhymes*

A Hyacinth in a Jar

(September to November)

You will need:

A small empty yogurt pot
A tallish glass jar (the smallest size of
   coffee jar is ideal)
A ball-point pen
A pair of scissors
A small piece of charcoal (see page 8)
A hyacinth bulb

You can grow hyacinth bulbs without soil or bulb fibre, as long as they are in contact with water; you can either buy a special hyacinth jar for this from a gardening centre, or make your own. The hyacinth bulb needs to have its root end resting in water, with plenty of room beneath for the roots to grow down.

To make your hyacinth jar, check that the yogurt pot will fit into the neck of the glass jar. Then draw a circle about the same size as the bottom end of the bulb in the base of the yogurt pot. Cut it out. (Ask an adult for help with this if you're not used to sharp scissors.)

Wash the glass jar, fill it with water and add a piece of charcoal, which will keep the water fresh. Rest the bulb and yogurt pot in the neck of the jar, so that the bottom of the bulb is in the water (you may have to make the hole in the pot bigger, if necessary).

Put the jar in a cool dark place until the roots growing into the water are about 10 cm (4 in) long and leaves are showing. Then move the jar into a warmer, lighter place, near a window.

Keep topping up the water so that the bulb is always resting in it, and enjoy the beautiful scent of your hyacinth.

Because the plant hasn't taken any food from the water, but used up its own store of nourishment, it won't grow again another year; throw it away after flowering.

A hyacinth jar

A home-made
hyacinth jar

A Flowering Tub

(September onwards)

You will need:

A wooden crate from a greengrocer's
    shop
A large sheet of heavy plastic
Scissors
About 20 tacks
A hammer
Broken crocks or smallish stones
Some pieces of charcoal (see page 8)
Compost
Bulbs (daffodils, narcissi, tulips,
    hyacinths or others), ivy and
    winter-flowering heathers
A watering-can

Ask your greengrocer if you can have
a crate that's finished with. With a
little help, you can turn it into an
outdoor container to brighten up your
porch or patio through the winter and
spring.

From *The Tale of Benjamin Bunny*

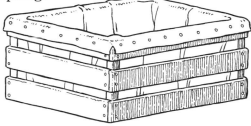

A flowering tub

First, line the crate with the sheet
of plastic (you can buy this from a
hardware shop if there isn't any going
spare at home). Trim the plastic as
necessary and fold a border over the
edge of the crate. With an adult's help,
hammer down the tacks to hold it in
place.

Pierce some drainage holes in the
bottom of the plastic with the scissors,
between the wooden slats. Lay some

broken crocks or stones in the bottom of the crate, for drainage, and fill it up with compost. (You'll need a lot of compost, which can turn out to be quite expensive, but it will give your plants the nourishment they need.)

Plant a selection of bulbs in the compost, pointed end up, following the instructions on the packet. Then group some winter-flowering heathers in the middle of your tub, planting them firmly in the compost when you have an arrangement you like. Add some ivy so that it trails over the edge of the container – perhaps cuttings you have taken (see page 26).

Water your tub well, and make sure it doesn't dry out through the winter months. In the spring, your bulbs should shoot up through the heathers and ivy to make a colourful display.

A Cress Hedgehog
(throughout the year)

You will need:

A hard-boiled egg
Cotton wool, kitchen paper or
   newspaper
Brown and black felt-tip pens
Brown or black Plasticine or
   modelling plastic
Cress seeds

Cress is delicious in sandwiches or salads, and it is fun to grow.

To make a hedgehog, cut a section off a hard-boiled egg, along its length. Scoop out the egg inside (use it in egg

From *The Tale of Mrs. Tiggy-Winkle*

A cress hedgehog

cut when they are about 5 cm (2 in) high.

You can also draw a face on an empty eggshell with the top sliced off horizontally. Stand the shell in an eggcup, fill the shell with wet cotton wool, newspaper or kitchen paper, and grow cress 'hair' on top above the face. To grow a larger crop of cress, sow the seeds in shallow trays (the foil containers from ready-made dishes are ideal), lined with a wad of wet kitchen paper or cotton wool. Again, keep the tray in a dark place until the seeds begin to sprout, then move it into the light.

sandwiches or kedgeree), and fill the shell with wet cotton wool, or pieces of wet kitchen paper or newspaper. Draw some prickles and a face on the eggshell with felt-tip pen, and add some Plasticine feet.

Sprinkle the cress seeds over the wet cotton wool or paper. Put the eggshell in a dark place until the seeds begin to sprout (about two or three days later), then move it into the light. Keep the cotton wool or paper damp, and the cress 'prickles' will be ready to

From *The Tale of Mrs. Tiggy-Winkle*

A Miniature Country Garden

You will need:

Some stones or a broken clay
flowerpot, for drainage
A fairly large bowl
Compost
A small mirror
White pebbles (perhaps from the
beach), or gravel
Some tiny rockery plants, such as
saxifrage, aubretia, alyssum, sedum
and thyme, or miniature trees

From *The Tale of The Flopsy Bunnies*

From *The Tale of The Flopsy Bunnies*

grown from fruit pips (see page 22)
A fine watering-can or sprayer, well-
rinsed if necessary
Some plastic animals, if you have
them

Lay the stones or broken crocks in the
bottom of the bowl and fill it up to
about 2 cm (1 in) from the brim with
compost.

Put your mirror on the compost, to
make a pond, and edge it with the
white pebbles or gravel. Then make

some paths with the pebbles or gravel, to divide your garden into sections.

Arrange the plants on top of the compost until you feel they look just right. You could put your little trees at the back of the garden, for example, and have one or two plants trailing over the edge of the bowl at the front, or you could group your fruit trees around the pond.

When you are happy with your arrangement, settle the plants into

From *The Tale of Tom Kitten*

hollows in the compost, and firm more compost around their roots. Water them well.

If you like, you can also put some plastic animals in your garden: a family of Puddle-ducks going down to the pond, for example, or some rabbits to nibble the plants, like naughty Peter and his cousin Benjamin Bunny.

Put your garden on a sunny window-sill, and water it whenever the soil dries out (at least once a week).

From *The Tale of Tom Kitten*

39

From *The
Peter Rabbit
Diary*

PROJECTS FOR WINTER

From *The
Tale of The
Flopsy Bunnies*

A Miniature Water Garden

(throughout the year)

You will need:

Two bowls, both fairly shallow, and
one about 4 cm (2 in) smaller than
the other, all round (a medium-sized
margarine tub is good for the inner
bowl)
Pebbles
Compost
Tiny plants, as listed on page 38, and
moss
A fine watering-can or sprayer, well-
rinsed if necessary
Some water plants, or 'aquatics',
which you can buy from a pet shop

From The Tale of Mr. Jeremy Fisher

Plants which grow in water are called
aquatics; they float on the water with
their roots hanging down. You can
make a lovely little indoor garden
using aquatics.

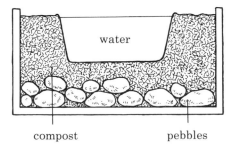

compost   pebbles

First, add a layer of pebbles to the
larger bowl and rest the smaller bowl
on top, so that they are more or less
the same height (top up with compost
if the smaller bowl is much shallower).
Then add more compost to fill in the
border around your pond.

Arrange some pebbles prettily
around your border, and fill the spaces
between them with moss and other
tiny plants. Settle the plants firmly
but gently into the compost when you
are sure you have the right place for
each one, and water them well.

Finally, put your aquatic plants into
the central pool, making sure not to
overcrowd it. Top the pool up with
water from time to time.

A Fairy Christmas Tree

You will need:

A small flowerpot
Some stones
A lump of Plasticine or modelling
    plastic (any colour)
A branch with several twigs coming
    out from it
Some old newspapers
Silver or gold spray paint
Several pine cones
Coloured paints
A paintbrush
Glitter
Thread
Scissors
Some wide red ribbon, if you have it

Although it doesn't grow, this tree looks very pretty on your window-sill or table at Christmas time. You can even tie small presents on it.

Wash the flowerpot, if it is dirty, and rinse the stones too. Put the stones in the pot and press a thick layer of Plasticine over the top. Stick your branch into the pot, adjusting it and the stones and pressing the Plasticine around it so that it stands up straight.

Put the pot on several sheets of newspaper and very carefully spray the branch with gold or silver paint so that it is evenly covered.

While the branch dries, paint the pine cones all over in different colours (you'll have to paint the tops of the cones when the bottoms have dried). While the paint on the tops of the cones is still tacky, lay them on some newspaper and sprinkle on glitter, to look like fairy snow.

When the cones and tree are quite dry, tie the cones on to the branches with thread.

Some wide red ribbon tied in a big bow around the pot finishes the tree off beautifully.

Watercolour for a Christmas card by
Beatrix Potter

43

A Bottle Garden

From *The Tale of Ginger and Pickles*

You will need:

A large clear glass or plastic bottle with a lid (you can use a sweet jar on its side, or a large pickle jar, or an old goldfish bowl with a cork to fit it)
A piece of paper
Some washed gravel

Some broken-up charcoal
Potting compost
5 canes or lengths of dowelling, about 30 cm (12 in) long
An old fork and spoon
A cotton reel or thread spool
A piece of sponge (if possible, soft natural sponge)
A nail
Some thin string
Scissors
Glue

Some small plants which won't grow too quickly, like tiny ferns, ivies and spider plants, and African violets
A pump-action sprayer, well-rinsed if necessary

A bottle garden is a good home for some plants, protecting them from draughts and dry atmosheres. Planting it can be quite fiddly, but, once you've finished this, your bottle garden won't need too much attention.

Wash out your container thoroughly. Then roll up the piece of paper to act as a funnel, and pour in the various layers of material in which the plants will grow: a layer of washed gravel for drainage, then an equal layer of charcoal pieces, then finally a layer of potting compost, about as

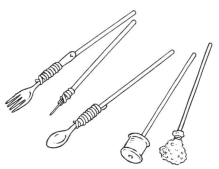

with the string. Then glue the cotton reel to another cane so that it is held firmly.

Dampen the sponge on its cane and use it to clean the inside of the jar, if it has become splattered with compost. Carefully dig small holes in the compost with the spoon and fork (use whichever is easier), in which to position your plants.

thick as the gravel and charcoal together. (You need to provide enough nourishment for the plant roots, but also room for the leaves and stem to grow.)

You will also need to make some special tools to reach down into your bottle. Tie the fork, the spoon, the sponge and the nail each to a cane

Take the plants out of their pots and, holding them by means of the nail on its stick plunged carefully into the root ball, lower them into their hollows in the compost. Heap compost around each one with the spoon, and firm it down with the cotton reel on its stick.

Clean the inside of the bottle with the sponge again, if necessary, and water the plants well with the sprayer. Seal your bottle garden with a cork or lid.

You don't need to worry about watering your bottle garden frequently. Just like the seedlings in their plastic covering, moisture evaporates through the plants' leaves, turns to water when it reaches the surface of the bottle, and trickles back down into the earth.

Don't put your bottle garden in direct sunlight, and keep an eye on the amount of condensation, or water droplets, on the inside of the bottle. If you can't see any at all, add some more water with your sprayer. If the bottle is streaming with moisture, leave the lid off for a day.

Index